# My WAGON Will Take Me ANYWHERE

by **Elizabeth Cody Kimmel** • *illustrated by* **Tom Newsom**

DUTTON CHILDREN'S BOOKS • NEW YORK

**For Emma Cody Kimmel,**
**whose imagination takes her everywhere**
E.C.K.


**To my son Andy**
T.N.

Published in the United States 2002 by Dutton Children's Books,

a division of Penguin Putnam Books for Young Readers

345 Hudson Street, New York, New York 10014

www.penguinputnam.com


Designed by Alan Carr and John Daly


Printed in Hong Kong


First Edition

ISBN 0-525-46721-1

10 9 8 7 6 5 4 3 2 1

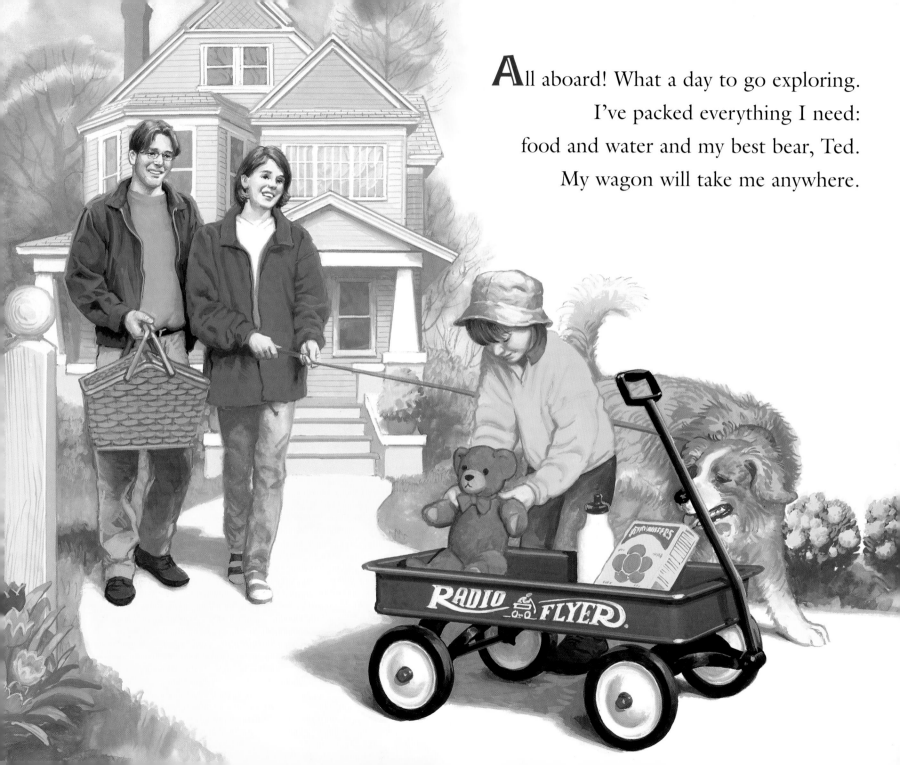

**A**ll aboard! What a day to go exploring.
I've packed everything I need:
food and water and my best bear, Ted.
My wagon will take me anywhere.

It's cold out this morning. Can that be snow?

Maybe it's really a blizzard!

Max, my sled dog, dashes and darts.

He'll stay on the trail through the storm.

Watch out for that water, Ted—don't fall in!

We're stuck on an iceberg, just floating.

Like penguins, we slither and slip and slide

as the polar bears wave good-bye.

It's much warmer here, on this jungle cruise.
There's a hippo right next to my boat!
He's grunting and growling and grinning so wide,
I wish we could take him along.

After months of sailing we've found the spot—
the island where treasure is hidden.
My first mate, Max, knows just where to dig.
We'll find glimmering, glistening gold!

The sun is bigger than I've ever seen it.
The desert burns, blazes, and bakes.
Ted and I rest in the shade of my tent,
then drink before we push on.

From here I can see the whole prairie.
I feel dusty and dirty and dry.
There's a buffalo running behind us.
Think he'll follow us all the way west?

Just a few more feet to the summit, Ted,
then we'll put down these heavy supplies.
Rocks crack, crumble, and crash below.
Better keep our eyes to the sky.

I'm at the controls on my way to the moon.

A comet shoots just overhead.

It whizzes and buzzes with fizzling sizzles.

Boy, am I glad it missed us!

There's nothing as fast as my red race car.

I scoot along speedy and swift.

The finish line's close, and the flag's in the air—

no one stands between me and first place!

I'm taking a trip on a night train,
snuggled safe in an upper bunk.
Out the window the world bumps by in a blur.
Who knows where we'll be when we stop?

This place is familiar. It's the best place of all.

It's comfortable, cheerful, and cozy.

Here's a soft bed and hugs and kisses good night.

Think I'll stay. Then tomorrow, who knows?

My wagon will take me anywhere.

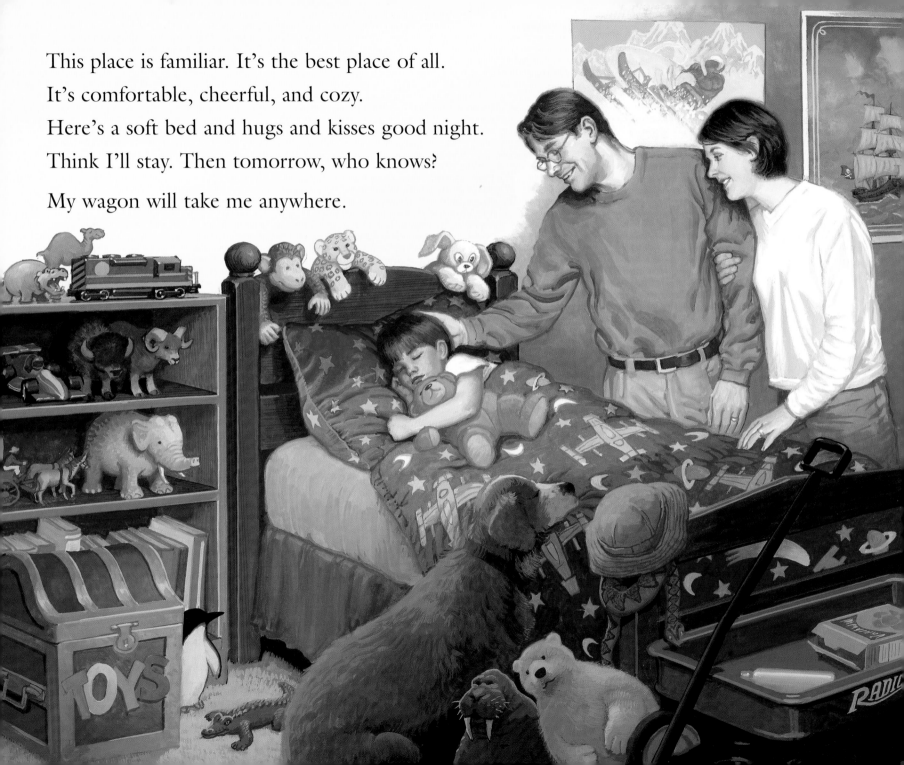